THE Wee Scot Book

Scottish Poems and Stories
Remembered and Illustrated by

Aileen Campbell

PELICAN PUBLISHING COMPANY
Gretna 1994

Published by arrangement with the author by
 Pelican Publishing Company, Inc., 1994
First Pelican edition, January 1994

*A treasury of remembrances of a childhood in Scotland
dedicated to my children*

---

*The word "Pelican" and the depiction of a pelican are
trademarks of Pelican Publishing Company, Inc., and are
registered in the U.S. Patent and Trademark Office.*

Library of Congress Cataloging-in-Publication Data

The Wee Scot book : Scottish poems and stories / remembered and
 illustrated by Aileen Campbell — 1st Pelican ed.
    p.   cm.
    Summary: An illustrated collection of poems and traditional tales
about Scotland.
    ISBN 1-56554-018-2
    1. Scotland—Juvenile poetry.   2. Children's poetry, Scottish.
3. Children's poetry, American.   [1. Scotland—Poetry,   2. American
poetry.   3. Scottish poetry.   4. Folklore—Scotland.]   I. Campbell,
Aileen.
PR8636.5.S36W44   1994
821'.008'09282—dc20   93-28728
                                                             CIP
                                                              AC

Manufactured in Korea
Published by Pelican Publishing Company, Inc.
1101 Monroe Street, Gretna, Louisiana 70053

CONTENTS

ACKNOWLEDGMENTS

I wish to thank: my husband **Bert J. McCausey,** who has been my support, critic and advisor; my sister, **Barbara Clark,** Lightwater, England; lifelong Scottish friend **Sheana Macleod,** Edinburgh, Scotland; **Dr. C. Allan Young,** scholar of Scottish culture and history; librarians, Pratt Library, Baltimore, Md.; and the Baltimore Gas & Electric Co., for research in old street lamps.

Acknowledgments are due and gratefully tendered to the following owners of copyrights, to publishers and other literary resources, for permission to include the following: "Skye Boat Song" by Harold Boulton from the **Children's Book of Scottish Ballads,** J. B. Cramer & Co. Ltd.; "Pussie at the Fireside" from the anthology **Scotscape,** Oliver & Boyd; "Highland Fairy Lullaby" Thomas Nelson and Sons Ltd.; "The Whistle" by Charles Murray, Charles Murray Memorial Trust; "Hallowe'en the Nicht O' Teen" and "Rise up Guid Wife and Shake yer Feathers" (Hogmonay) from **The Lore and Language of School Children** by Iona and Peter Opie (1959), Oxford University Press; and "Birds at the Fairy Fulling," "Land of Heart's Desire," and "Kishmul's Galley" from **Songs of the Hebrides** by Marjory Kennedy-Fraser, Boosey and Hawkes.

I also wish to thank the following for research of copyright restrictions: Central Library, **George Fourth Bridge,** Edinburgh, Scotland; British Copyright Council, London, England; Performing Right Society Ltd., London, England; Galaxy Music Corporation; **William Rossa Cole,** Hanson Music Company; and Library of Congress.

While every effort has been made to trace copyright owners, the publishers apologize for any omissions in the above list.

Aileen Campbell

The Cover

My grandson Alistair is pictured as a piper on the cover. He was born with the pride of Scotland in his heart. At an early age, he could recognize "Scotland The Brave," a tune that appealed to him so much, that he learned to imitate the sound of the bagpipes when the pipers played the song. With his homemade whistle, he blew until his cheeks puffed out alarmingly. The melody droned through his closed nostrils while he tapped his foot to the familiar beat. This wee lad felt the fire of pride as he marched to the Scottish rhythm.

The castle in the background is Kilchurn. It stands on a promontory at the end of Loch Awe, connected to the shore by a stretch of marshy land. After having made a pilgrimage to Rome, Sir Colin Campbell, known as the Black Colin of Rome, occupied the Castle around 1440. During one of his absences, his wife, Lady Margaret Stewart of Lorn, rebuilt the Castle.

Kilchurn Castle has been a ruin for many years, but historical places such as this will be long remembered through their stories.

Aileen Campbell

To My Reader

Come follow my path through the
pages of this book, to a land rich in
sentiment and history. The old songs
of Scotland may be new to your ears
but they are easy to dream over. Deep
down in the soul of your being, there
is a spirit that will lighten to the
lilt of the words.

As you wander through the pages
I hope you will hear the call of the sea,
smell the scent of the peat and
bog-myrtle and, envision the purple
of the heather hills.

Where the dialect is strange to you,
sound it slowly and hear the music

in the words. Like the prattle of mountain streams, and the lap of the tide on the shore, there is a lilt to the Scottish tongue. Try it, and savour it ~ you will find there is an appealing rhythm to your speech.

And now, curl up in your favourite corner and lower the lights. Turn the pages slowly, listen to the fairy music and 'wi' heather honey taste upon each name,' journey on to dreamland.

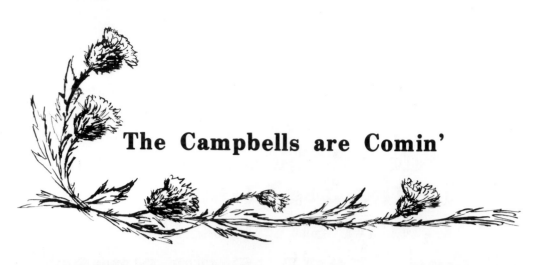

The Campbells are Comin'

Found in many old Scottish song books, "The Campbells are Comin'" is a well-known march originally called "Baile Inner-aore" in Gaelic "The Town of Inverary." It is considered "a Campbell tune" and was the review march for the First Battalion Argyll Regiment and Sutherland Highlanders, formerly the Ninety-First Highlanders.

The words were written to music in about 1715. The composer is unknown, but some speculate that it may have been one of the Duke of Argyll's common soldiers.

Peoples the world over have marched and danced to the catchy tune and easy beat of "The Campbells are Comin." The repetition of the the lines proclaim the importance of the Campbells' arrival at Loch Leven.

The Cambells are coming
O ho, O ho!
The Cambells are coming
O ho, O ho!
The Campbells are coming
to lovely Loch Leven,
The Cambells are coming
O ho, O ho!

Upon the Lomonds I lay, I lay
Upon the Lomonds I lay, I lay
I looked down to lovely Loch Leven
And saw three lovely perches play.

The Campbells are Comin'

The Campbells are comin'
Oho, Oho!
The Campbells are comin'
Oho, Oho!
The Campbells are comin'
to bonnie Loch Leven,
The Campbells are comin'
Oho, Oho!

Balavil Song

This story, like a fairy tale, should begin "long, long ago" because the song and pictures were inspired by the author's life in Balavil, Ross-Shire, Scotland, many years ago. "When I was a young girl, I lived in an old farm house. The back windows of our house overlooked the other farm buildings and the hay-strewn cobbled yard where the cows trudged from the byre (barn) to the pasture, and back again. By the creaky garden gate, the flowers bunched, eagerly reaching for the sunshine. The oats were stored in the stockroom at one end of the house and the pungent odor of grain flooded the room above. I wrote verse there by candlelight or played music on an old phonograph or just dreamed dreams."

Balavil was situated in the Black Isle, a fertile farming area in the northeast of Scotland. Although it is called the Black Isle, it is not actually an island. It is dark in appearance because of the forested land that faces the Moray Firth.

A steady climb eastwards from Balavil ends in a stretch of small farms. A reward awaits the enduring walker: to the west the hills of the Wester Ross stand proudly on the skyline. The scenic beauty and the stillness of the quiet countryside instill peace in those who live in Balavil.

Balavil Song

When evening shadows fall,
And swallows homeward fly,
The sunny day has passed away,
And cloudlets fill the sky.

The bees have long since gone to rest,
And the sun dips to sleep,
The weary bird has sought its nest,
And shepherds tend their sheep.

Through cirrus cloud the moon appears
A large and wistful ball,
And stares across the stubble fields
Whereon the brown leaves fall.

Aileen Campbell

The Lamplighter

This nineteenth century poem was written by Robert Louis Stevenson (1850-1894). When the poet was a child, he did not enjoy good health, and spent many days in bed. While there, he created imaginary adventures among the hills and valleys of his coverlet.

The warm glow of the lamp would cheer the spirit of any lonely boy that gazed at the lamplighter. While "leerie" actually means lamp, it is the affectionate name Scots give to a lamplighter.

The Lamplighter

Now Tom would be a driver
And Maria go to sea,
And my papa's a banker and rich as he can be,
But I, when I am stronger,
And can choose what I can do,
O Leerie, I'll go round at night
And light the lamps with you.

R.L.Stevenson
from "The Lamplighter"

Poussie at the Fireside

In Scotland, a picture of a cosy cottage with a cheerful fire glowing in the fireplace would never be complete unless it showed a cat comfortably asleep on the fireside rug.

In this poem, the pussy is allowed to eat its oatmeal on the hearth rug instead of in the kitchen. A hot cinder pops out of the fireplace and lands on the poor cat's nose. She must have been too close to the fire! The cat complains, "That's nae fair!" and runs away in pain. The cinder warns that she should not have been there, (but in the kitchen).

This rhyme was chanted by Scottish children when one of their friends fell or hurt themselves because of carelessness.

Poussie at the Fireside,
Lapping up his oatmeal
Down came a cinder,
And burnt pussy's nose
"Oh!" cried pussy,
"That's not fair!"
"Well," said the cinder
"You should not be there!"

BROSE
A handful oatmeal
pinch of salt
mix with boiling water
to desired thickness
sup with cream

Pussie at the Fireside
Suppin up brose
Doon cam a cinder,
An' burnt pussie's nose
"Oh!" cried pussie,
"That's nae fair!"
"Weel", said the cinder
"Ye sudna be there!"

The Lea-Rig

When o'er the hill the eastern star
Tells the homing of cows is near, my jo;
And oxen from the furrowed field
Return so sad and weary, O.

Down by the stream, where scented birches
With dew hang clear, my jo;
I'll meet you on the lea-rig,
My own kind dearie, O.

In darkest glen, at midnight hour
I'd rove, and never be eerie, O;
If through the glen, I went to you,
My own kind dearie, O.

Although the night was so wild
And I was never so weary, O;
I'd meet you on the lea-rig,
My own kind dearie, O.

The Lea-Rig

When o'er the hill the eastern star
Tells bughtin-time is near, my jo;
And owsen frae the furrow'd field
Return sae dowf and wearie, O:

Down by the burn, where scented birks
Wi' dew are hangin' clear, my jo,
I'll meet thee on the lea-rig,
My ain kind dearie, O.

Robert Burns

In 1787, Robert Burns wrote to the Noblemen and Gentlemen of the Caledonia Hunt announcing his call to "sing in his country's service, to be acknowledged as a Scottish bard and lay his songs under their protection."

The elder son of a landowner's servant and a struggling farmer, Burns was "bred to the plough." He knew hard labor and the constant threat of financial ruin. But he continued to write, his words seeming to flow effortlessly and he produced hundreds of poems, letters, and songs. Ill health consumed Burns and, in 1796, at the age of 37, one of Scotland's brightest lights went out.

How well Burns wrote of rural Scotland! With the first verse of "The Lea-Rig," Burns paints a scene of peaceful beauty. The eastern star faintly shimmers above the dimming countryside, day is gently caressed to dusk, and the cows' soft mooing heralds their coming from the fields to the "byre" for milking. The sculptured white trunks of the "birks" (birches) define the lea-rig, a small uncultivated strip of land amidst the ploughed fields.

Each year more people learn to appreciate Burns' poetry. In commemoration of his birthday, special celebrations called "Burns Suppers" are held worldwide on January 25th. At the Supper, the traditional country haggis or oatmeal dish is "piped" in with much fanfare. In honor of the occasion a Scottish piper leads the procession and with crossed swords on either side, the silver platter is regally carried forth. A dignitary, or one who can sport a good Scottish brogue, reads Burns' famous salutation, "Address to the Haggis," while he proceeds to carve its "entrails bright," and acclaims, "O what a glorious sight, warm reekin, rich!"

Burns' songs fill the air in the musical program that follows, and toasts ring out in praise of Scotland's beloved poet.

Years ago, "Burns Suppers" were only celebrated by men. But when the author was a girl, the annual "social," a village concert, welcomed all. It was held during the bleak winter months and everyone gladly sang the "auld Scottish Songs;" including many of Burns' poems, favorites that had been set to music. In fact, the tenor at one Burns celebration was the author's father. Well does the author remember how he stood with head back, eyes closed, and hands clasped together, while rendering "The Lea-Rig, Aye Fond Kiss, Bonnie Wee Thing" in a sweet voice. During intermission, over cups of steaming hot teas and sticky buns, old friendships were renewed and new ones made.

When the final song was sung, the door was opened to the chilly blast of the night air. But, there at the door, was the "pokey," a final farewell. The pokey, given to every child, was a goody bag with an orange and apple. And so, fortified with the nostalgia inspired by Burns' music and the pride of kinsmanship, the long walk home was begun with remembered gratitude to our Scottish Bard Robert Burns.

The Three Craws

Crows are frequently represented with a sinister tone in Scottish rhymes and folk tales. Remembered as wily predators, crows rob the eggs from momentarily unprotected nests.

This rhyme reminds the author of the crows seen as she walked down the country road to school in winter. In her young eyes, the crows were her inspiration to sing this rhyme while she skipped and played along the three-mile walk to school.

Three crows sat upon a wall,
Sat upon a wall, sat upon a wall,
Three crows sat upon a wall,
On a cold and frosty morning.

The first crow could not fly at all.
Could not fly at all, could not fly at all,
The first crow could not fly at all,
On a cold and frosty morning.

The second crow fell and broke his jaw,
Fell and broke his jaw, fell and broke his jaw,
The second crow fell and broke his jaw,
On a cold and frosty morning.

The third crow was crying for his Ma,
Was crying for his Ma,
The third crow was crying for his Ma,
On a cold and frosty morning.

The fourth crow was not there at all.

The Three Craws

Three craws sat upon a wa',
Sat upon a wa', sat upon a wa',
Three craws sat upon a wa',
On a cold and frosty morning.

The Whistle

This true gem of poetic appeal is by Charles Murray. It is often memorized and considered a legacy to all Scots.

The story begins with a young farmhand who carves a simple whistle from a rowan tree branch. His love of Scottish traditional music causes him to neglect his chores, for which he is duly punished, but he finds comfort in his whistle.

While the reader can taste the traditional food and feel the warmth of kindly folk living a modest country life, there is the penetrating cold of winter, the pain of punishment, and the insensitivity of the master. When the last powerful verse is read, a hush follows the loss of the whistle.

He cut a green shoot
from the large Mountain Ash
he trimmed it, and he wet it,
and he thumped it on his knee;
he never heard the lapwing
when the harrow broke her eggs.
He missed the crested heron
catching frogs in the marshes,
he forgot to hound the collie
at the cattle when they strayed,
but you should have seen the whistle
that the young ploughboy made!

The Whistle

He cut a sappy sucker
From the muckle rodden-tree,
He trimmed it, an' he wet it,
an' he thumped it on his knee;
He never heard the teuchat
when the harrow broke her eggs,
He missed the craggit heron
nabbin' puddocks in the seggs,
He forgot to hound the collie
at the cattle when they strayed,
But you should hae seen the whistle
that the wee herd made!

He whistled all the morning
and he tooted all the night,
he puffed out his freckled cheeks
until his nose sank out of sight,
The cows were late for milking
when he led them up the lane,
The kittens got his supper then,
and unfed, he was sent to bed;
But he cared not a bit
What they did or thought or said,
There was comfort in the whistle
That the young ploughboy made.

For lying late the mornings
he had cleaned the bowl for weeks,
But now he had his bonnet on before
The others donned their trousers;
he was whistling to his porridge
That was cooking on the fire,
he was whistling through the stalls
to the foreman in the barn
Not a blackbird nor a thrush,
That had whistled all the day,
Was an equal to the whistle
that the young ploughboy made.

He played a march to battle,
It came sounding through the mist
Till the farmhand squared his shoulders
and made up his mind to enlist
he tried a song for wooers,
Though he did not know its meaning,
But the kitchen lass was laughing
and he thought she maybe knew;
he got cream and buttered round cakes
For the loving lilt he played.
Wasn't that a cheery whistle
That the young ploughboy made?

He blew those tunes so lively,
Scottish dances, reels and jigs,
The foal flung his large legs
and capered over the ridges,
The gray-tailed weasel peeped out
to hear his own strathspey
The hare came leaping through
The corn to "Clean Pease Strae,"
The feet of every man and beast
got itchy when he played—
have you every heard a whistle
like the young ploughboy made?

But the snow it stopped the herding
and the winter brought him grief
When in spite of hacks and chilblains
he was sent again to school;
he could not recite the Catechism
nor count the rule of three,
He was punished and kept in the classroom
when the other boys went home;
But he often played the truant—
'Twas the only thing he played
for the master burned the whistle
that the young ploughboy made!

...The Whistle

He wheepled on't at mornin'
an' he tweetled on't at nicht,
he puffed his freckled cheeks
until his nose sank oot o' sicht,
The kye were late for milkin'
when he piped them up the closs,
The kitlins got his supper syne,
an' he was beddit boss;
But he cared na doit nor docken
what they did or thocht or said,
There was comfort in the whistle
that the wee herd made.

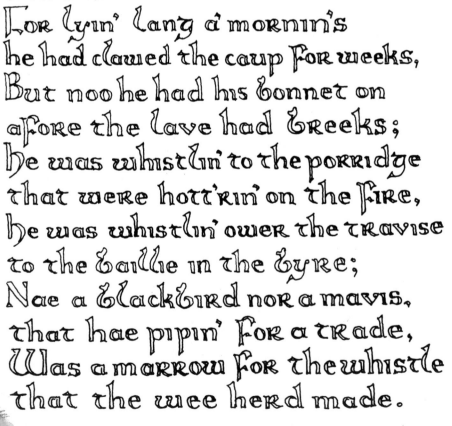

For lyin' lang a' mornin's
he had clawed the caup for weeks,
But noo he had his bonnet on
afore the lave had breeks;
He was whistlin' to the porridge
that were hott'kin' on the fire,
he was whistlin' ower the travise
to the baillie in the byre;
Nae a blackbird nor a mavis,
that hae pipin' for a trade,
Was a marrow for the whistle
that the wee herd made.

...The Whistle

He played a march to battle.
It cam' dirlin' through the mist.
Till the halflin squared his shouders
an' made up his mind to 'list;
He tried a spring for wooers,
though he wistna what it meant,
But the kitchen-lass was lauchin'
an' he thocht she maybe kent;
He got ream an' buttered bannocks
for the lovin' lilt he played.
Wasna that a cheery whistle
that the wee herd made?

He blew them rants sae lively,
schottisches, reels, an' jigs,
The foalie flang his muckle legs
an' capered ower the rigs,
The grey-tailed futtrat bobbit
oot to hear his ain strathspey,
The bawd cam' loupin' throuch
the corn to "Clean Pease Strae,"
The feet o' ilka man an' beast
gat youkie when he played—
hae ye ever heard o' whistle
like the wee herd made?

...The Whistle

But the snaw it stopped the herdin'
an' the winter brocht him dool,
When in spite o' hacks and chilblains
he was shod again for school;
he couldna souch the Catechis
nor pipe the rule o' three,
he was keepit in an' lickit
when the ither loons got free;
But he aften played the truant—
'twas the only thing he played,
For the maister brunt the whistle
that the wee herd made!

Charles Murray

Poussie, Poussie, Baudrons

"Poussie, Poussie Baudrons" is the Scottish version of the English nursery rhyme, "Pussy Cat, Pussy Cat, Where Have You Been?" The English version was first published during the reign of Queen Elizabeth (1558-1603), while the Scottish version was first published in "Songs for the Nursery" in 1805 and in other Victorian publications (from 1837—1901).

In the Scottish version illustrated here, Baudrons—an affectionate name for a poussie or pussy cat—watches the mouse run up the stair, rather than under the Queen's chair as in the English version. Finally, the captured mouse is put in the cat's "meal-poke" or food bag, to be eaten later.

"Pussy, pussy, baudrons,
Where have you been?"
"I've been to London
To see the queen."

"Pussy, pussy baudrons,
What got you there?"
"I got a good fat mouse,
Running up a stair!"

"Pussy, pussy baudrons,
What did you do with it?"
"I put it in my meal-poke,
To eat with my oatcake."

Poussie, poussie, Baudrons

Poussie, poussie, baudrons,
Whaur hae ye been?"
I've been tae London
Tae see the Queen"

"Poussie, poussie baudrons,
Whit gat ye there?"
"I gat a guid fat mousike,
Rinnin' up a stair!"

"Poussie, poussie baudrons,
Whit did ye dae wi' it?"
"I pit it in ma meal-poke,
Tae eat tae ma breid".

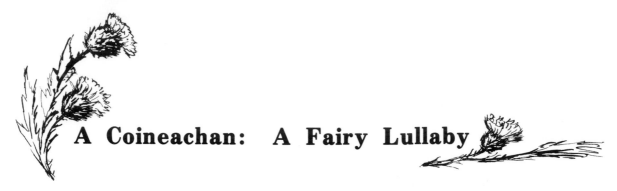

A Coineachan: A Fairy Lullaby

I left my darling lying here,
Lying here, lying here;
I left my darling lying here,
To go and gather blaeberries.

I found the track of the yellow fawn,
The yellow fawn, the yellow fawn;
I found the track of the yellow fawn,
But could not trace my baby, O!

I found the trail of the mountain mist,
The mountain mist, the mountain mist;
I found the trail of the mountain mist,
But never a trace of baby, O!

Hovan, hovan, Gorry og O,
Gorry og O, Gorry og O,
Hovan, hovan, Gorry og O,
I've lost my darling baby, O!

This Gaelic lullaby from the Hebrides tells a story of Celtic folk lore. The tale warns that if a baby is left unattended and alone, the fairy folk may steal it away and leave a "changeling" in its place.

In "An Coineachan," a mother busily gathers blaeberries on the hillside. (Blaeberries are not blueberries, but a small, tangy berry found in quantity in Scotland.) So intent is the mother at her work, that she has momentarily forgotten her baby. But that is all the time the fairy folk need to snatch away her wee one. It was believed that fairy folk stole unattended babies and left "changelings" in their place. When the mother looks for her baby, no trace does she find. By following the track of the yellow fawn and the trail of the mountain mist, she searches but never finds her baby.

Her Gaelic lament "Hovan, hovan, Gorry og O" reminds the Islanders as they sing to watch over their babies.

Translated from the Gaelic by Lachlan MacBean.

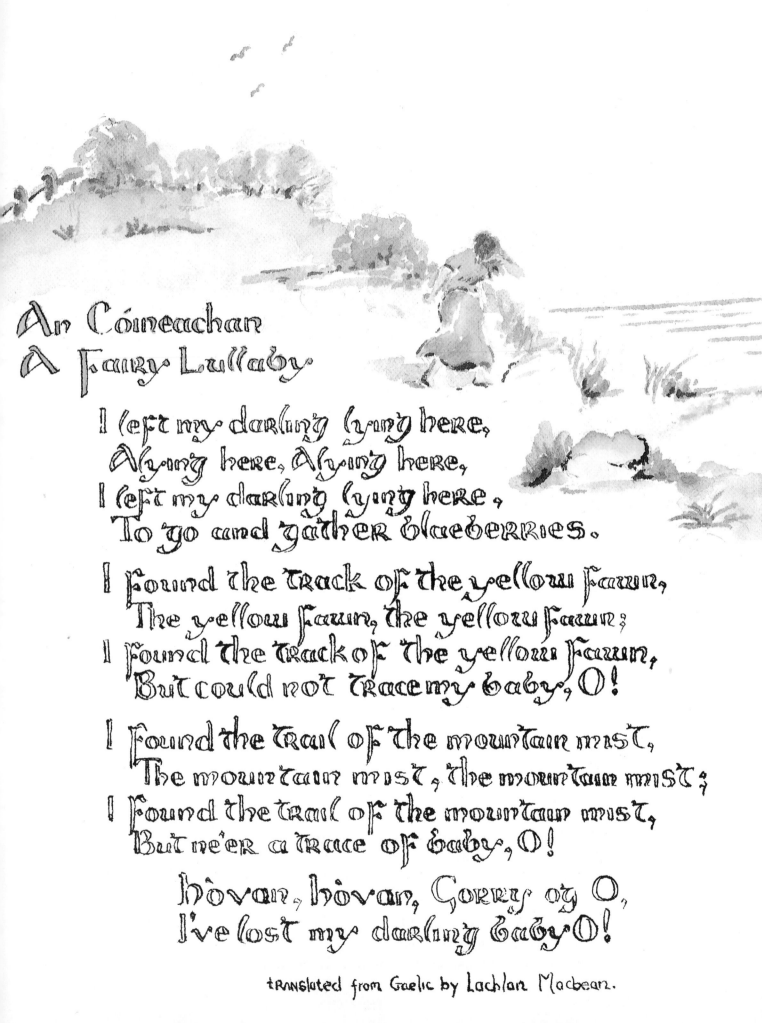

An Cóineachan
A Fairy Lullaby

I left my darling lying here,
   A-lying here, A-lying here,
I left my darling lying here,
   To go and gather blueberries.

I found the track of the yellow fawn,
   The yellow fawn, the yellow fawn;
I found the track of the yellow fawn,
   But could not trace my baby, O!

I found the trail of the mountain mist,
   The mountain mist, the mountain mist;
I found the trail of the mountain mist,
   But ne'er a trace of baby, O!

hòvan, hòvan, Gorry og O,
   I've lost my darling baby O!

translated from Gaelic by Lachlan Macbean.

Coulter's Candy

Ally-bally-bally-bally-bee,
Sitting on your mommy's knee.
Crying for a wee half-penny,
To buy some Coulter's candy.

Poor wee thing, you're looking awful thin,
A handful of bones and a wee bit of skin.
But soon you'll have a small double chin,
From sucking Coulter's candy.

"Coulter's Candy" is a children's folk song, but is enjoyed by all ages for the memories it evokes.

It is believed that Mr. Coulter peddled candy in the town of Kelso, near the border between Scotland and England during the late nineteenth century.

Candy, commonly called "sweeties" in Scotland, is still sold in "sweetie" shops today in most towns and villages. But it was probably no easier for a child to choose candy from Mr. Coulter's store than to make a selection from the many brightly colored sweeties in the glass jars of the sweetie shop.

Coulter's Candy

Ally-bally-bally-bally-bee,
Sittin' on yer mammy's knee,
Greetin' fer a wee bawbee
Tae buy some Coulter's candy.

Puir wee thing yer lookin' awfu thin,
A puckle o' banes and a wee bit skin,
But soon ye'll hae a wee double chin,
Frae sookin' Coulter's candy.

The Craws

The crows have killed the kitten, O!
The crows have killed the kitten, O!
The large cat sat down and cried
In Jeannie's small house, O!

This is one of the old Scottish ditties that should be recited in a "broad Scot" dialect. Recite it aloud with expression, savoring the words.

In many Scottish homes the windows do not have screens. On warm days, the windows are left open to enjoy the fresh breezes. Visitors are often warned not to leave their gold jewelry in view because the crows will steal anything that shines, especially gold.

As mentioned previously, the crows are always thought to be the cause of destruction. Here, the mother cat, a fine calico color, cries for her kitten.

The Craws

The craws hae killed the pussie, O!
The craws hae killed the pussie, O!
The muckle cat sat doon and grat
In Jeannie's wee bit hoosie, O!

Wee Willie Winkie

This nursery rhyme, always a favorite, has been recited throughout the years to entice children to bed. Still, "sax (six) o'clock" seems rather early for even young children.

William, Prince of Orange, who later became King William III of England, was nick-named "Wee Willie Winkie." He was an advocate of "early to bed, early to rise" and this theme influenced the rhymes of a number of children's poems written at this time.

William Miller quoted the rhyme in his book "Songs for Nursery," Number 1, composed around 1844. It was published earlier in the "Whistle Binkie" collection by David Robertson.

Wee Willie Winkie
Runs through the town,
Upstairs and downstairs
in his nightgown.
Rapping on the windows,
Rattling all the locks;
Are the wee ones in their beds?
For now it's six o'clock!

Hey, Willie Winkie,
Are you coming within?
The cat's purring
beside the sleeping hen,
The dog's stretched out on the floor
and doesn't make a sound,
And I have a sleepless lassie
Who will not fall asleep.

Anything but sleep, you rogue!
Glowing like the moon,
Rattling like an iron jug
With an iron spoon.

Rumbling, tumbling round about,
Crowing like a cock;
Screaming like "don't know what,"
Waking sleeping folk.

Hey, Willie Winkie,
The wee one's in a hamper!
Sliding off a person's knee
like a very eel,
Pulling at the cat's ear,
and ruffling all her hair—
Hey, Willie Winkie—
See, here he comes!

Wee Willie Winkie
Runs through the town,
Upstairs and downstairs
in his nightgown.
Rapping on the windows,
Rattling all the locks;
Are the wee ones in their beds?
For now it's six o'clock!

Wee Willie Winkie
Runs thru the toon

Upstairs and
Doonstairs
in his nicht goon
Rappin' on the windaes
Tirlin' at the locks

Are the weans
in their beds
For noo it's
sax o'clock!

Wi' A Hundred Pipers

With a hundred pipers and all, and all,
With a hundred pipers and all, and all,
We'll up and give them a blow, a blow,
With a hundred pipers and all, and all,

Oh, it's over the Border away, away,
It's over the Border away, away,
We'll on and we'll march to Carlisle Hall
With its gates and castle and all, and all.

"Wi' A Hundred Pipers" celebrates Prince Charles Edward Stuart's capture of Carlisle in his effort to regain the throne of Great Britain. Prince Charles, known to the enemies of the Stuarts as "the Young Pretender," and as "Bonnie Prince Charlie" to his supporters, was the grandson of James II who was deposed and banished to France with his son James, the "Old Pretender." Thus, the Protestant Hanovarian succession to the throne of Great Britain was not threatened. Stuart supporters were known as Jacobites (from the Latin Jocobus for James) and longed for the return of Prince Charles from France so that he could regain the throne of his ancestors.

In 1745, with only seven men and borrowed funds, Prince Charles landed on the west coast of Scotland. Once there, he organized over one thousand men willing to join his fight. Because the regular Scottish army was stationed in Inverness, the thousand marched through Perth and Edinburgh unchallenged. Then, when they crossed the river Esk into England, the Prince and his men, now over five thousand strong, captured Carlisle.

When the city gates of Carlisle were opened, one hundred pipers heralded the victorious Prince and his men. To commemorate the victory, Lady Nairne wrote the four verse ballad, "Wi' A Hundred Pipers."

Meanwhile, Prince Charles had marched to within 120 miles of London, but retreated when it became evident that he did not have the support needed to win the battle. The rebellion ended at the Battle of Culloden in which Prince Charles lost over one thousand of his loyal followers.

The Hundred Pipers

Wi' a hundred pipers an' a', an' a',
Wi' a hundred pipers an' a', an' a',
We'll up an' gie them a blaw, a blaw,
Wi' a hundred pipers an' a', an' a',
Oh, it's ower the Border a-wa', a-wa',
It's ower the Border a-wa', a-wa',
We'll on and we'll march tae Carlisle ha'
Wi' its yetts and castle an' a', an' a'.

Lady Nairne

Birds at the Fairy Fulling

In the glade of this Hebridean Island, it is the time for the "fulling of the cloth," a vibrant activity involving the women of the Island.

In this poem fairy folk were involved. The cloth was thickened by the process called "fulling" or "waulking." An even number of workers sitting around a wattle board would tug and pull on the cloth, rotating it clockwise with a rhythmic motion to evenly stretch and finish it. Working songs lightened this tiresome work. As they pulled and turned the cloth, they would sing a song in the rhythm of their work.

In this song, the workers are fairies and birds. The fairies promise the birds a special feast if they will help with the work. Above the flutter of the wings the fairies call, "Hey blackbird, haste to our feast" and "Ho lintie (or linnet) add to our glee." Imagine a bright tartan stretched and tossed in the breeze until the cloth, now thickened and shrunk, is ready for wearing. Then off to the fairy feast of fruits and nuts laid out for the birds on a circle of toadstools.

Hey, blackbird hasten to our feast,
Sing, while we toss, at least,
Ho feerum forum fo, ho fara can an clo'.

Ho, linnet add to our glee,
Tell whose the plaid shall be,
Ho feerum forum fo, ho fara can an clo'.

Ho! thrush whistle and call,
To whom the plaid may fall
Ho, wing and feather and song,
Toss 'til the web is strong.

Ho, feerum forum fo
Ho fara can an clo',
Heart's love to a little fairy woman
Well know she whose (plaid) it will be!

BIRDS
at the Fairy Fulling

Hey! blackbird, haste to our feast,
Sing, while we toss, at least,
Ho feerum forum fo, ho fara can an clo..

Ho! lintie add to our glee,
Tell whose the plaid shall be,
Ho feerum forum fo, ho fara can an clo

Ho! mavie whistle and call,
To whom the plaid may fall
Ho, wing and feather and song,
Toss 'till the web is strong.

Ho, feerum forum fo
Ho fara can an clo,
Heart's love to Benakshee,
Well knows she whose 'twill be!

When The Kye Comes Home

James Hogg wrote this pastoral poem in the late eighteenth century. He was a shepherd from the small village of Ettrick and was known thereabouts as the "Ettrick Shepherd."

Many Celtic rites and customs were built around the shepherd and his flock. Sometimes the shepherds played whistles while caring for their sheep and dreamed of their bonnie lassies. In the highlands of Scotland, the herding tunes were songs of the people who sent their sheep to graze on the hillsides.

The melody of "When the Kye Comes Home" stirs childhood memories for the author. The song was whistled by a favorite uncle, who was often heard on the country road long before he was sighted.

Come all you jolly shepherds
That whistle through the glen
I'll tell you a secret
That courtiers do not know.
What is the greatest bliss
That the tongue of man can name?
It is to woo a bonny lassie
When the cows comes home,
When the cows comes home
Between the twilight and the dark
When the cows come home.

When The Kye comes home

Come all ye jolly shepherds
that whistle through the glen
I'll tell you a secret
that courtiers do not ken
What is the greatest bliss
that the tongue o'man can name
'Tis to woo a bonny lassie
When the kye comes home.

The Skye Boat Song

Prince Charles Edward Stuart, known as Bonnie Prince Charlie, and his valiant followers were defeated at the battle of Culloden in 1746. The Prince escaped from the battlefield, although many died as they wielded their claymores or heavy two-handed swords. Bonnie Prince Charlie wandered through the Highlands until a clever plot allowed his escape from Scotland.

People could not travel about easily during these times of strife. But Prince Charlie found an escape when Flora Macdonald, whose father was the captain of an independent shipping company, arranged a visit to her mother on the Isle of Skye in the Inner Hebrides. Flora was allowed the accompaniment of a single serving maid. Prince Charlie was that maid in disguise.

Some Scots see a hint of romance between Flora and the Prince, but sentimental endearments were only a part of the song. Flora married one of her clansmen four years after Prince Charlie fled from Scotland. Never again did the Prince pursue the throne of his ancestors.

Speed, Bonnie boat,
Like a bird on the wing,
Onward, the sailors cry;
Carry the lad
That is born to be king
Over the sea to Skye.

Loud the wind howls,
Loud the waves roar,
Thunder claps rend the air;
Baffled our foes stand on the shore;
Follow they would not dare.

Many's the lad, fought on that day
Well the claymore did yield,
When the night comes
Silently lay
Dead on Culloden's field.

Though the waves leap,
Soft shall ye sleep:
Ocean's a royal bed;
Rocked in the deep,
Flora will keep
Watch by your weary head.

Harold Boulton

Baloo Baleerie

Baloo baleerie, baloo baleerie,
Baloo baleerie,
Baloo balee.

Go away little fairies,
Go away little fairies,
Go away little fairies,
From our cosy cottage, now.

Down come the lovely angels,
Down come the lovely angels,
Down come the lovely angels,
To our cosy cottage, now.

Sleep softly my baby,
Sleep softly my baby,
Sleep softly my baby,
In our cosy cottage, now.

Fairy people, called "wee folk," are part of Celtic folklore. Babies were traditionally rocked to sleep while listening to stories of the fairies. Better to be asleep than to hear the fairies scurry about later, disturbing the darkness.

"Baloo Baleerie," a favorite lullaby because of its gentle rhythm, tells of the coming of the "bonnie angels" who restore a heavenly peace for baby's sleep until dawn breaks over the hills.

Baloo Baleerie

Gang awa' peerie fairies,
Gang awa' peerie fairies,
Gang awa' peerie fairies,
Frae oor ben noo.

Baloo baleerie,
Baloo balee.

Doon come the bonnie angels,
Doon come the bonnie angels,
Doon come the bonnie angels,
Tae oor ben noo.

Baloo baleerie,
Baloo balee.

Sleep saft my baby,
Sleep saft my baby,
Sleep saft my baby,
In oor ben noo.

Baloo baleerie,
Baloo balee,

Hallowe'en

All Hallows Eve or Hallowe'en is on October 31st, the day before the beginning of the Scottish winter. As night approaches, the imaginations of those celebrating this age-old custom lengthen like the shadows at the wane of daylight. After all, the soft darkness may be partially concealing a witch as she scurries to find her broomstick and join the other sorcerers in their dance on the village green.

On the hilltops, large bonfires are lit to chase away spell-casting spirits. Farmers secure their carts, ploughs, and other tools to prevent them from being carried away.

As superstition died out in Scotland, pranksters continued the work that had earlier been feared of the spirits. Those who grumbled seemed to suffer the more next year round.

The screeching owl intensifies the sinister appearance of the dancing witches, but the warm glow from nearby jack-o'-lanterns dispels the fear on All Hallows Eve.

Halloween the night of grief,
Three witches on the green.
One black and one green
And one crying halloween.

halloween

Halloween the nicht o' teen,
Three witches on the green.
Ane black an' ane green
And ane cryin' halloween.

I remember Scottish Hallowe'ens, when I was a little girl, because I grew up on the Brahan estate, in the north of Scotland.

The evening meal was a hurried one on Hallowe'en night because we had to put the finishing touches to our make-believe costumes. Dressing up as a witch was a favorite one. It was easy to find an old black skirt and shawl in these days. If we wanted a "false face," we had to save our pennies and walk three miles to the village where, if we were lucky, we would find one in the "shoppie," or store as we now know it. So we usually used homemade disguises to change our appearance. Soot, from the chimney was great, with a few dabs of flour here and there for added touches.

Brahan was a perfect setting for ghoulish fun. It was an estate, complete with castle and its own ghost. The maids in the castle showed me the ghost's bedroom. It was an ordinary-looking room, but when they found the bedcovers folded down every morning as though someone had slept in the bed—well, something was out of the ordinary. Peggy, the housemaid, told me privately she had pinned the bedspread up on the pillows, but still the covers were pulled down!

Then there was the Brahan Rock, a wooded rocky hill lying to the north. Weird moaning sounds could be heard in the still of the night coming from its direction. Some folks said the rock was an old volcano rumbling. Wildlife could also be heard rustling in the underbrush. Often the quiet was broken by another loud crack when a stag struck his antlers on a tree trunk.

The few children who lived in Brahan gathered in small groups to go "trick or treating." We may have looked scary, but many times we shivered in our boots at a strange noise. The roads were lonely because the houses were a good distance apart. Familiar scenes became unfamiliar, even in the bright moonlight. The flickering turnip lanterns that we had carefully carved out of large "neeps," or as we now know them as large turnips, made even more eerie shadows around us.

Dressed up in our special disguises on Hallowe'en, we were known as the "guisers." Knocking on the cottage doors, we felt quite brave shouting, "trick or treat!" But the challenge was to go to the castle and brave that old ghost! We had to pass the farm buildings and the garages where the gentry's Rolls Royce and Mercedes cars were housed. We then could see the castle looming ahead of us. We would carefully tiptoe, holding our breath until we got to the back entrance. The thump of the huge old knocker usually brought Helen, the housekeeper. She liked the guisers to visit the servants and always treated us royally. But, she also liked us to perform for our treats; so maybe a bold witch among us would give out a few screeches and howls, brandishing her broomstick! Our pokey-bags would then be filled with goodies, which we carefully measured out for the days ahead.

One Hallowe'en, when our guiser group visited the castle, the servants had set a large washtub in the servants' hall. There, they had placed the reddest of apples floating on the water. We were invited to dunk for apples and dunk we did, trying to catch an apple with our teeth. If we succeeded, and succeed we did, we kept the apple and were told we would have good luck for the whole of the next year! I don't remember if that came true, but I do remember that there were several wet and bedraggled witches and gypsies that night! But our treat bags were full and I do believe the happy night was never forgotten.

From ghoulies and ghosties and long-legged beasties
And things that go bump in the night,
Good Lord deliver us.

Kishmul's Galley

Centuries ago, on the Island of Barra in the Outer Hebrides, a great castle stood on a rocky promontory in Castle Bay. The castle, called Kishmul or Kisimul, was the stronghold of the Macneills, who were descendants of the son of Neil, King of Ireland.

Kishmul's Galley is an excellent example of a "waulking" or working song. The song celebrates the bravery of the galley crew, who, as defenders of the castle, are returning against wind and tide. But galleys were also used for plundering expeditions among the islands of the Hebrides.

The first verse creates a setting from which the reader views the galley's struggle to return to the castle, described in the second verse. In the concluding verse, the crew safely reaches the castle's shore.

The original poem, believed to have been written by the Barra poet Nic Iain Fhinn, had the typical rhythm of a working song. Some documentation suggests, however, that the verses were written by a Mrs. Maclean of Barra. In a later arrangement, Marjory Kennedy-Fraser gave the song a flowing, ballad style.

High from the hill in Barra,
On a day of days—
Seaward I gazed,
Watching Kishmul's Galley sailing.
O-hi-ho-huo, fal-u-o

Homeward she bravely battles
'Gainst the hurtling waves,
Nor hoop nor yards,—
Anchor, cable, nor tackle has she.
O-hi-ho-huo, fal-u-o

Now at last, 'gainst wind and tide
They've brought her to
'Neath Kishmul's walls,
Kishmul Castle, our ancient glory
O-hi-ho-huo, fal-u-o

Kishmul's Galley

High from the Ben a Hayich,
On a day of days –
Seaward I gazed,
Watching Kishmul's Galley sailing.

Homeward she bravely battles
'Gainst the hurtling waves,
Nor hoop nor yards, –
Anchor, cable nor tackle, has she,

Now at last, 'gainst wind and tide,
They've brought her to
'Neath Kishmul's walls,
Kishmul Castle, our ancient glory.

Hogmonay

Hogmonay is actually the Scottish name for New Year's Eve. Scots, too, ring out the old year and ring in the new, but with different customs. In some areas of Scotland, on Hogmonay, children dress up as they might elsewhere for Halloween and sing or dance for favors from their neighbors.

One custom, the "first footin," is based upon the belief that the coming year will bring good luck and full larders if a dark-haired person is the first to cross the doorstep after the stroke of midnight. A "first-footer" usually carries a lump of coal or peat and a gift of food to signify plenty.

The author's mother, who had dark brown hair, was always the first-footer in their house. Just before the stroke of midnight, she would leave by the back door with the lump of coal and a large basket of goodies. Then, at the last stroke of twelve, there was a tap, tap, tap on the door and the dark-haired woman would "first-foot" their home. Throughout the countryside, the distant sound of bells rang in the New Year.

Rise up good wife and shake your feathers,
Do not think that we are beggars,
We're just children out to play,
Rise up and give us our hogmonay.

Hogmonay

Rise up good wife and shake yer feathers,
Dinna think that we are beggars,
We're just bairns cam oot to play,
Rise up and gie's oor Hogmonay.

Dream Angus

The musical words of this old Gaelic lullaby by George Churchill soothes like the steady rhythm of an old rocker over scrubbed wooden floors. The mother cradles her babe near the flickering light of the fire; she sings and rocks, sings and rocks. The wee one is restless and does not quieten. "A' the wee lambs are sleepin', birdies are nestlin', nestlin' the gither," the mother's soft voice croons, but her baby is slow to hush.

Then she gathers her shawl about the wee one to soothe and quiet. When "Angus is here wi' dreams to sell," the promise of dreamland is now so close. Angus, the Scottish sandman, comes to all drowsy children with the promise of refreshing sleep. Over the hills and through the heather he goes, not a whisper of sound to be heard, so that the little ones can be rocked to sleep.

Can you no hush your weeping?
All the wee lambs are sleeping;
Birdies are nestling, nestling together
Dream Angus is slowly, slowly walking over the heather.

Dreams to sell, fine dreams to sell,
Angus is here with dreams to sell,
O! hush you my baby and sleep without fear
Dream Angus has brought you a dream my dear!

List to the curlew crying!
Fainter the echoes dying,
Even the birds and beasties are sleeping
But my pretty baby is weeping weeping.

DREAM ANGUS

Can ye no hush yer weepin'?
A' the wee lambs are sleepin',
Birdies are nestlin', nestlin' the gether
Dream Angus is hirplin' owre the heather.

Dreams to sell, fine dreams to sell,
Angus is here wi' dreams to sell.
O! hush ye my baby and sleep without fear
Dream Angus has brought you a dream, my dear!

List to the curlew cryin'!
Fainter the echoes dyin',
Even the birds and beasties are sleepin'
But my bonnie bairn is weepin' weepin'.

George Churchill

At Eventide

Sunset in promise of a bonnie morning;
Peace on the waters where the cobbles ride;
And a few old skippers snoozing in the twilight
Waiting to go out on their last high tide.

In the Scottish fishing villages, a group of weathered-looking "worthies" are usually gathered under the shelter of the sea wall. They speak softly in a dialect that is often barely understandable to born and bred Scots, unless from the east coast.

The "cobbles," flat-bottomed boats, set out at eventide for a night's fishing. Some of the old skippers watch the boats fade from view with a longing to go out to sea and cast their nets as in the olden days.

"Sunset in promise of a bonnie mornin" is a poetic description of the saying: "Red sky at night is the shepherd's delight." Fishermen, like shepherds, expect fair weather on the day following a red sunset. But a rosy sunrise forecasts rain so the rhyme concludes: "a red sky in the morning is the shepherd's warning." And when the sun's last rays shed a golden glow over the land and sea, it is the gloaming, that mystical twilight between day and night. In the gloaming, the old skippers wait to go out "on their last high tide."

TRAVISE: division between stalls
WA: wall
WAMBLIN': sliding
WAUKENS: awakens
WAULKING: working, or "shrinking the cloth"
WAUPS: curlews
WEAN: child, wee one
WEE: small

WEE COT: cottage
WHAUR: where
WHEAN or *WHEEN:* few
WHEEL: well
WI': with
WINDAES: windows
WINNA: will not
WINTIN': wanting (without)

WIS: was
WISTNA: did not know for sure
WOO: to court
WOOERS: lovers
YER: your
YETT: gate
YOUKIE: unable to sit still, itchy

Dreams

And so you have been led on a mystical journey through Scotland. You have heard the old songs of the Isles, listened to the proud tunes of the clans, shared the ballads and lullabyes, and smiled at the wee ones' rhymes.

Throughout Scotland dialects are forever changing. I have tried to share some of these with you.

Perhaps this journey was to the land of your birth, or maybe you were a visitor to Scotland, searching for kinfolk or sentiment. I trust your yearnings have been fulfilled and that someday you will visit again in person, not as a stranger, but as a family coming home.

AILEEN CAMPBELL

Pause a moment on this mossy bank,
Whisper your dreams.
Bluebells will listen and nod
In the gentle breeze.